INFINITE

Victor Cabinta

INFINITE
VOL. I

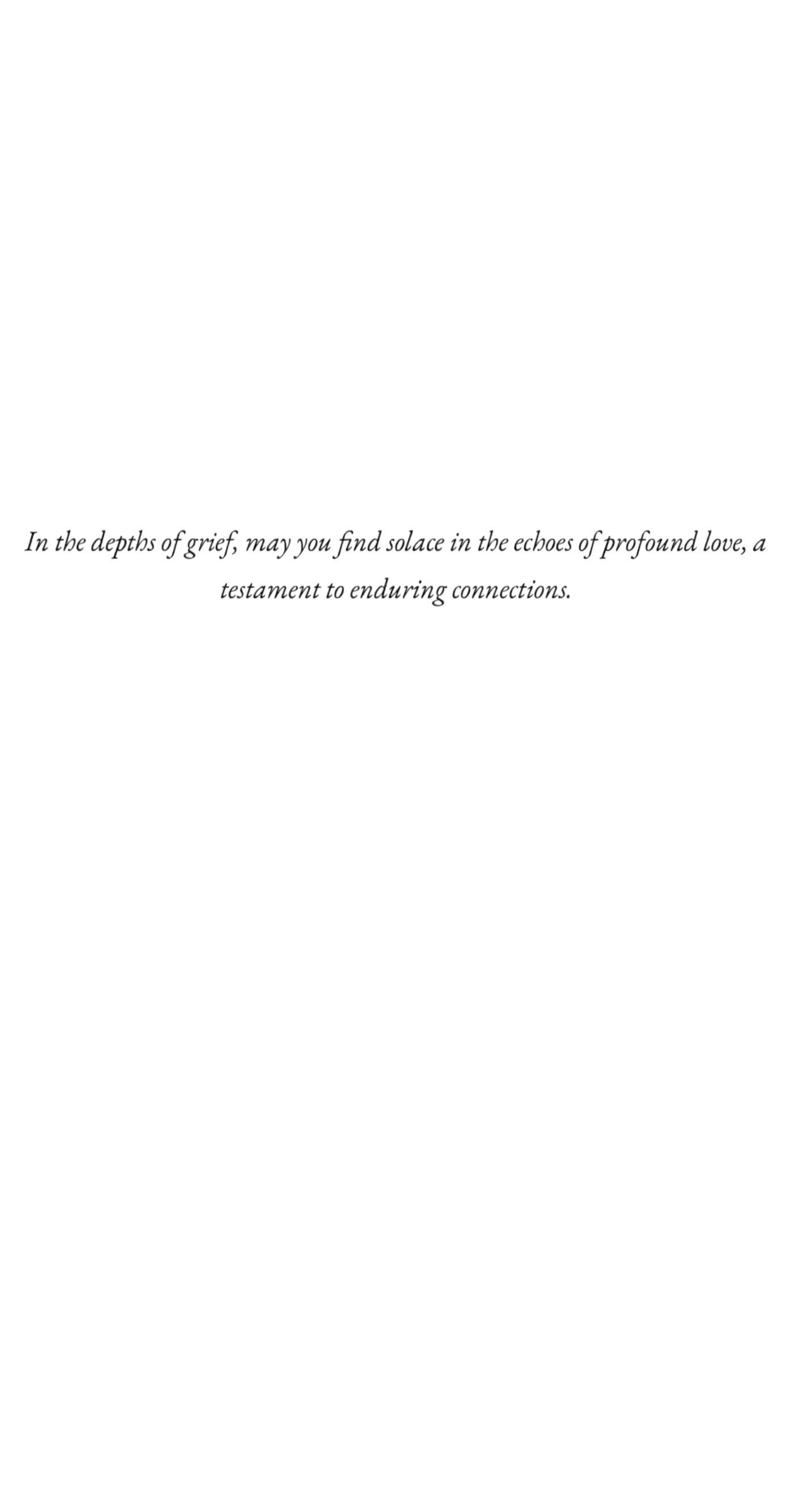

In the depths of grief, may you find solace in the echoes of profound love, a testament to enduring connections.

Introduction

Dear Reader,

In assembling this collection of short stories, I initially didn't discern a common thread among them. Yet, as I reflect, an unintentional but poignant theme emerges. Each narrative, in its own way, delves into the intricate dance of emotions that define our human experience. In the words of Vision, "What is grief if not love persevering?" As you traverse these tales, may you find solace and resonance in the unspoken connections that bind us all.

Love, Victor Cabinta.

MAGIC SHOP

The Magic Shop will comfort you

Perspective

Two weeks, two damn weeks since I broke my right leg. I fucking hate this. I sit here with nothing to do in this four-walled room like a prisoner. No, that's too harsh. It's pretty much a five-star service here. My relatives do a lot for me, but I can't help but be angry. It's not VJ's fault my tibia almost fell out of its socket. We rehearsed our exit blocking for weeks, but things happened so fast on that stage and we collided.

The cracking sound resounds in my head and I shake away the memory. I lie back down on the bed, but really, it's just a futon. It's honestly really comfortable for the cast. I knock on it twice and it's still solid as a brick. I miss my friends. I miss school. And I miss dancing. My phone buzzes, it's Kirk.

WE MISS YOU!

Hey Kirky, miss you guys too :(

Stop being sad, bitch! You're literally on vacation.
BE GLAD!

You right :p

I was just with your Aunt. I gave her your hw.

Thanks!

How's the leg?

Still broken :((

Dw Vic, you're gonna get better and dance again

Idk about that. The doctor said this ends my professional dance career. Sigh.

Angie and I are coming!

No! No need! I love you guys! <3

I put my phone down. Kirk and Angie are tremendous blessings in my life. They are easily one of the most incredible people I've met in the Philippines, who are now part of my circle of friends who become family. But I really don't want them here right now. It'd just remind me of the biggest setback in my life. They were there when it happened. I remember them both vaguely looking from afar when I was getting placed on a gurney.

I groan. My left hand searches for my earphones on the side of the bed. I find it, plug the cord into my phone, and play a random song. I make myself comfortable and close my eyes. If I just sleep now, I won't think about it. The next song plays and immediately my eyes open wide. "Bitch." I exasperate. Our competition song plays. Never have I ever pressed the "next" button so fast. I'm trying to not have nightmares!

∞

"Hoy! Wake up!"

That sounds like Angie.

"Hoy!"

My bed shakes and my eyes open. "What the fuck?" I sit up. "You guys are really here."

"Duh, I told you we were coming." Kirk laughs.

"How did you guys even get in?" I scoot to the side to make space and lean my back against the wall. My leg now rests on the tiles.

"Your Aunt I think? She said we can come up." Angie takes off her huge purse.

"Wow, thanks, family. They could have sent murderers up here for all I know." My face scrunches.

"It's a good thing we aren't that." Kirk grins.

I throw him a pillow. "You're so funny. Sit down hoes. Plenty of space in my humble abode."

Both of them place their bags against the closet and sit down on the futon/bed. Angie sits between Kirk and me. I abruptly scoot to my right and a sharp pain riles up from my leg to my hips. I groan.

"You okay?" Angie looks at my leg.

"Yeah, I moved too fast." I breathe deeply, trying to keep my composure.

Silence fills the room.

"Vic, did you watch the new PLL episode?" Kirk leans forward and looks at me, breaking the silence.

"No, I don't have time."

"Oh. I have it if you want?" He keeps his stare.

I look down and nod, "Uh yeah, sure."

"This is so weird." Angie takes a pillow and hugs it.

"What is?" I turn my head to her.

"You." She furrows her brows.

I say nothing and look back at my cast.

"I don't like you defeated. You're the one who told me not to let anything take me over." Angie says calmly but I know what scolding is, and this is just a milder version of it.

"Yeah Vic, you're always the positive one. Remember in dance class? You helped me overcome my shyness, and taught me to always look at the positive things." Kirk adds.

"How is this positive? I just lost everything that's me."

"It isn't the end though, Victor. You know you'll dance again, just let yourself heal." Angie holds my hand.

"No..." I shake my head, "This is literally the end for me Ange." My hand pulls away from hers.

Kirk moves to the edge of the futon by Angie's legs and faces me.

"All I have was this. When shit hits the fan or when I—" I take a deep breath in and exhale. "When the overthinking takes over, I would dance it out. It helped release a lot of the bullshit, you know. But now?" I point at my leg.

"You don't know that," Kirk says.

"I do though!" That came out louder than I expected. "I'm gonna be waiting for that fucking cracking sound again and— fuck." I turn away looking up, hoping none of my tears fall.

"Oh, Vic." Kirk moves in front of me, sitting on his knees, and starts rubbing my back.

"Eww! I'm crying." I laugh and wipe my tears. "I'm sorry guys."

"No, it's alright." Angie's hand lands on mine again and this time I accept it. "You're a talented writer, you still have that."

"That's for a career, dancing is my passion."

"Then make writing a passion too," Kirk says still rubbing my back.

I shrug. "Look, I don't expect you guys to understand. When I'm on stage for the next three to five minutes, I'm somebody else. It sounds really dumb but in those five minutes, I become someone who's not insecure or afraid of what people say about them because I am, all the time. When I'm up there, I feel like the best me, the confident me, the one who's positive like you said." I look at Kirk and pause. "The doctor said I can't become the dancer I want to be. There's a chance if I blow my leg out again, it can be permanent so, yeah," I look at Angie, "I'll heal and dance again but there's that limit now. What do I do knowing that?" My voice cracks.

Kirk and Angie don't say a thing. All they do is embrace me, and my head buries into Angie's shoulder. After weeks of being numb, I finally weep. I don't want to be mad, I'm far from it. I'm sad. I can't accept it, I don't think I'll ever accept this. How could I be so careless?

I knew the dance, how could I space out and forget our exit? All these questions pile over me like a tidal wave of ultimate regrets. My biggest regret was overestimating my strength.

∞

Two Months Later

"Are you sure you're ready to go back to school?" Tita Alyn says with her hands crossed, for sure thinking I'm crazy for wanting to go back when my leg hasn't recovered yet.

"Yes, Ta," I side-eye her. *Do you guys expect me to stay in bed for another few months?*

"Okay, balong." She finally agrees. "But if your leg starts hurting, you come home, okay?"

My grip tightens on the handles of the crutches. "Yes, I'll call right away." I put all of my weight against it and push myself forward with my left leg. I propel myself with each step to the van.

"We're leaving now?" Tito Rey walks over to me and slides the door open. He helps me into the van by holding onto my waist and slightly carrying me in. I sit on the chair and let out a huge sigh. That was so much work. He places my crutches on the car floor.

"Thanks, Tito."

He nods. The van's engines come to life. My auntie waves and I wave goodbye back. The drive to UC is about fifteen to twenty minutes. Since we moved to where we live now a year ago, I can finally say I experienced living in the mountains. The roads are extra bumpy, not to mention the near heart attacks I get from seeing how narrow the roads are. I don't trust the railings that separate us from the cliffs.

Baguio always looks good in the morning. Angie and Kirk are waiting for me, they want to drop me to my classes, and as much as I don't want any physical help, I miss them so much. The whole ride was quiet. I look at my cast and knock on it, still rock solid. The doctor said maybe in a week I can finally get rid of the thing but I'm honestly not ready to walk. That cracking sound scares the hell out of me. We hit a pothole and I bounce up.

My leg feels that sting again and I gasp.

"Sorry!" Tito Rey raises his right hand and looks at me through the rear-view mirror.

"I'm okay, Tito." I smile at him but really, that was terrifying. We get to school and I spot Kirk and Angie right away. Kirk with his blonde comb-over isn't really hard to miss and Angie has a particular stance that signifies it's her, that, and her glasses. These two were a plot twist, after one of our classes ended two semesters ago, they invited me to hangout at Kirk's place and what was supposed to be just a karaoke night became a whirlwind of drunk thoughts, crying sessions, and one of the best nights I ever had in the Philippines. So glad they thought I was cool. Tito parks the van in front of them and Kirk slides open the door.

"Hi!" Kirk greets me. "Hello, po." He looks to Tito Rey.

"Hello po, Tito." Angie approaches the van.

"Hi, guys," I soft smile.

"Oh, hello. John, do you need help?" Tito Rey looks at me.

"It's okay po. We got him." Kirk tells Tito Rey and reaches for my hand.

Angie takes my crutches. I pull myself out of the van and Kirk holds onto my waist tightly. My working leg searches for the ground. I feel it and place all my weight on that leg, dragging out my cast and gently placing my toe on the ground. I'm so happy I wore black socks.

"Here." Angie hands me my crutches and I find my balance.

Kirk slides the van door close and we wave goodbye to Tito who honks at us.

We watch the van leave and a cold breeze pelts our skins, Angie's hair flowing with it. We look at each other, let out a chuckle, and go for a group hug.

"I missed you guys." I squeeze tighter.

"Ange and I are so bored in class. We always go to the canteen to buy the fries you like," Kirk says.

We let go of our embrace.

"Oh man, I miss Potato Corner." I place the right crutch under my armpit and rub my stomach.

"Don't worry, we'll buy some for you after we drop you," Angie says wrapping her arms around mine and leaning her head on my shoulders.

I press my head on hers.

"Okay, let's go so you can sit down." Kirk takes my backpack and holds it for me. The walk through the main building, past the engineering building to the G buildings, was a nightmare. I'm so happy elevators were going down to my class because the stairs would have gotten me to call Tita Alyn. Speaking of stairs, everyone had their eyes on me. I mean, I would stare at a person with a cast covering their entire leg. A few of my friends and classmates saw me along the way and congratulated me for getting third place in the competition, would've been first if I hadn't blown my leg out.

∞

Six days would have passed since my return to the Uni. I don't know how people who have to go through this their whole lives, adapt because I certainly have not. My armpits are sore from the crutches. I had the height for them wrong in the first place. My nurse sister finally tells me that the crutches aren't supposed to be touching my armpits. Would've been nice to know two months ago!

I found a faster route to my classes and I stopped meeting with Kirk and Angie every time I arrived at school. I love their help and will forever be grateful but if they continue to treat me like I'm wounded, I'll stay like that. This cast comes off tomorrow so I want to show them I can do this. With that being said, I'm here alone in class, and the first one the past few days. This gives me a lot of time to think, which I really shouldn't be doing because lately, I've only been thinking about bad things. I feel the shift and the acceptance of it all. Everything feels so dull now that dancing isn't my everyday routine.

I take out my phone and check my photo library. There it is, it's even the thumbnail for the folder. I click the album and the last video I have is of the competition. My index finger hovers over the video for a few seconds. I haven't watched the performance yet. Kirk recorded it from the bleachers and gave the video to me on my first day returning. I press on it and the video begins playing. The first part of the dance was the choreography I made for my dance crew in Guam, Team Alumni.

This dance started a lot of opportunities for me and ironically, started this set of the competition piece. Yet, Fate, Vj, Lean, and I were chosen for this set specifically by our director. I feel a soft smile cracking on my face. I see the appeal, we all have similar styles, plus the song is the most different in genre throughout the set. The next dance is the quick feet set and the five of us weren't a part of it, which was a bummer because I really love this dance. Man, I'm getting so hyped watching this, I can still feel the thrill of it all. The third set is the Beyonce dance I made. 7/11 is a masterpiece of a song and everyone was a part of this, even the boys!

I swear after the boys saw me in the Vogue/Wacking set last year, they all wanted to be a part of this too. As they should! This was a really powerful performance from everyone. I just remember during rehearsals I'd die out in this section. It really was heavy in energy and I was scrunching all of mine during it. I look around to see if anyone is coming and watch me bop my head profusely. The fourth dance is the jazz piece with all the jazz-trained dancers, four of them.

I applaud them all, I would have joined this set too if it weren't for me catching my breath, my life. Changing into the next costumes was really hard. This year, our college went bigger with props and costumes, which meant plenty of helpers backstage with the dancers, hence the claustrophobia. Trying to catch my breath and having to put my clothes on, is way harder than you think. My smile fades as I watch the last set of our comp piece come to place. This is it, this is where I broke my leg. I pull the phone closer to me, my elbows leaning against the desk.

My heart starts racing. My palms sweating. I focus on myself, watching me give my all when in the next few seconds, my whole life is going to be altered. Here it comes, I see myself running to leave the stage and VJ crossing my way too but what I didn't realize was a third person was running in the same direction as us. In a split second, all three of us collide with each other, and in a flash, I hear the cracking sound resounding in my ear. I jolt in my seat, dropping my phone on the desk. I look around to see if anyone is here, none. But everything I lost is.

Throughout the day, I kept quiet and my distance from everyone. I can see it in everyone's face, how wounded I look to them, and they're not wrong. I would have never lashed out at my friends but today was bad. I'm in my last class and I dread going home. I pull out a folded piece of paper and re-read it. It took a while to write but I finished it in class this morning. I fold it back and put it in my pocket.

Watching that video was a mistake because I'm so angry. I hate this, this isn't me, but I'm so tired. I'm tired of the "I'm sorry, Victor" from everyone. I'm so tired that anything people talk to me about is my leg and the painful reminder that I won't dance the same anymore. I'm so tired of faking my feelings because if I say what I really feel, everyone will think I'm being dramatic, but don't I deserve to be? I'm never gonna be a professional dancer, why is that not valid?

Angie leans to me, "Victor, we're going to SM after class. We'll wait for Tito Rey with you."

Kirk turns around to me, "Yeah, we don't mind." He smiles.

"No, guys it's okay." I shake my head. "I can do it myself, you guys go enjoy."

"Let us walk with you outside at least." Angie frowns.

"No, really. I'm gonna stay in here to catch up on some homework. I can't focus at home." I lie.

"You sure?" Kirk furrows his brows.

"Yeah."

Kirk and Angie look at each other.

"Okay." Angie nods and squeezes my arm.

An hour passes and everyone leaves the room. Angie and Kirk hug me and I give them the biggest one. They look back at me before leaving and I smile big, waving like I'll never see them again. They leave and I wait about ten minutes before I get up with my crutches. I drag myself to the elevators and as I get there, all that can come out of my mouth is, "Fuck." A big sign that reads OUT OF ORDER is plastered on the doors of the elevator. I have to take the damn stairs.

The stairs here lead to the nursing building, which will take me directly outside, whereas if I go the other direction, it's to the engineering building and then the canteen that would lead to the other exit of the building. But that's so much further and the stairs cut that by ten minutes. I got this. I head for the stairs, eyeing the flights—three more floors to climb. Let's just get through this. Grabbing my left crutch, I push down on the first step. Oops, wrong hand. I try to pull back, but it's too late. Losing my balance, I start plummeting to the ground. A scream escapes, but it's cut short as I hit the floor. Left arm takes a hit, right foot rises and slams down. Fuck.

I yell in agony as my right leg shoots a pain worse than ever. Clutching my leg, I bite my lip, tears streaming down. Suppressing my scream, I scan the empty building. "Help! Anyone, please!" My voice cracks, echoing in the silence. Releasing my leg, I lie on my back, letting the pain numb me.

No one's coming. No saving me this time. The pain eases after a few minutes of just lying here. Sitting up, I wince from the fall's sting on my arm. I stretch for my crutches, pausing to collect myself. Inhaling deeply,

I lean on the wall for support. Another jolt of pain in my leg makes me groan, but I manage to haul myself upright.

Inhaling deeply, I crouch to snatch my crutches. "I fucking got this." Tears stream down my cheeks as I grip both crutches in my right hand, propelling myself up with my left against the wall. Reaching the landing, I pause, catching my breath before tackling the next flight. This time, fatigue sets into my right hand from the strain. Almost there, just one more flight, and I'll hit the main floor. Mustering all my energy, I ascend these fucking stairs.

Reaching the summit, the crutches slip from my grasp, and I slump against the wall. My heart threatens to break out of my chest. Letting out a deep sigh, I stoop to retrieve the crutches, and that's when the faint strains of music catch my ears. I guess my heartbeat was the concert because the music is coming from CAS. It's the new main office for the College of Arts and Sciences; the nursing office relocated two floors above me. Clutching the handles, I drag myself closer.

The only one inside seems to be the secretary. Miss Agnes used to work for the Alumni Department before transferring to my college. Peeking in from outside, I see her behind her desk, engrossed in watching a group of Asian singers. The song is catchy, yet soothing, almost like I want to contemplate life. Even though the lyrics aren't in English, I get the vibe they're aiming for. I pull away and head for the exit. Dusk embraces me with its chilly winds, and I spot Tito Rey waiting at the other entrance.

He pulls the van in front of me and helps me down the stairs. I fucking hate stairs.

Decisions

I sit here in this four-walled room with nothing to do. After everything, after being helpless, I don't need to put myself through that anymore. I dig into my pockets and take out the folded letter. I need to hear myself say it out loud:

Dear Family,

I'm sorry. I love you all. I don't know if there's anything out there for me anymore, or if I can continue living like this. I'll be "good as new" but the damage of it all, mentally, can't fix me. Thank you for being the best and most supportive family that I could have. Tell my friends I love them and to not be sad. Maybe wherever I go, I'll be dancing. Think of me that way.

Tell Papa and Mom that they are the best parents, even though I fight with them a lot. Tell Ling and Jun that having them as my big brother and sister was the best because they're my first best friends. Tell Shawn and Roshelle I'm so happy I gained an extra brother and sister. I loved our childhood. Tell Raven, my baby sister, to keep being herself, because she's going to be the best of all of us. And finally, please, no burial, I want my ashes to be with the sea. Thank you guys, I'm sorry it ended this way, please forgive me.

Love, Victor John

The heaviness enters my chest and I weep. I don't want to go but I can't do this anymore. Everyone keeps saying it'll get better but what is my life if the one thing that brings me joy is taken away? Who will I be? I close my eyes and try to calm myself. I can't let myself cry, I need to do this. The melody from that Asian group comes to my head and I focus on that.

I start humming, and for a split second, I kind of regret what I'm thinking of doing. I open my eyes. "What fucking song was that?" I drop the letter on the floor and open my laptop. I Google, "Asian group songs" and shit, that was so broad. What the fuck was that song, it's going to make me crazy. I look back at the letter and wipe my tears.

I groan. I can postpone a day, I just need to hear that song one more time.

I get to school and hurriedly drag myself to CAS' main office. It's busy today, well, then again it's the morning. I crutch my way in and this is the first time I'm here on my accord. My eyes widen and I smile as I see the secretary. I hurry to her and she turns around.

"Hello, Miss Agnes?"

"Yes?"

"This is going to be so random, but um- yesterday, I heard a song you were playing around 7 PM, and I'm just curious about what it was?"

"Oh, that was Magic Shop by BTS."

"BTS?"

"A K-Pop boy band. You're Victor right?"

"Yes." I nod.

"You did really good for us. I'm sorry you're going through that." She looks at my leg, "But you are so talented. You remind me of one of the members of BTS."

"Really? Who?"

"His name is Jimin." She opens the browser on her desktop and goes to YouTube. "Here, sit down." She pulls an extra chair out under her desk.

I sit.

"My bias is RM." She smiles.

"Whose that?"

"He's the leader of the group, they call him rap monster."

"Oh, I get it, RM." I nod. "Magic Shop you said?"

"Yes, that's from their Love Yourself album."

Love Yourself? Is that why it made me feel a certain way? "What's it about?"

"It's a love letter to their fans. We're called ARMY because BTS stands for Bullet Proof Boy Scouts."

"Oh, that's cool."

"Yes, Magic Shop is about the fans, telling us to be the best for ourselves, because we make them the best they are."

"Wow, I love that." I smile.

"Here, let me show you Jimin." She brings up a video. For the next two hours, I would watch, listen, and become an ARMY. I would get my cast taken out, start walking regularly, and start training again for next year's competition. The letter? It got buried under my bed and eventually, I threw it out. Miss Agnes, who I now call my *Omma*, gave me something that day, hope. She also gave me BTS who without a doubt saved me.

Magic Shop became my anthem. Dancing is never the same but I can't give up on it, and myself. I owe it to the five-year-old who dreamt big to get to where I am today. I am a dancer and I'll be one for the rest of my life. But, my Magic Shop opened to let writing be a passion rather than just a career. Someday, I'll be able to tell this story, and maybe, I can be the person to pass down the bulletproof vest as my *Omma* did for me.

LAPERA
Pandesal

∞

Filipino (Tagalog & Illocano) Vocabularies

1. **Pandesal [pan·duh·saal]**: a bread roll

2. **Lolo [low·low]**: Grandpa

3. **Kuya [koo·yuh]**: a male who is older than you and closer in age

4. **Ading [ah·ding]**: someone younger than you (illocano)

5. **Walis tingting [wuh·list·ting·ting]**: broomstick made from coconut midribs

6. **Taho [taa·how]**: snack food made of fresh soft/silken tofu, syrup (sweetener and flavoring), and sago pearl

7. **Balut [buh·loot]**: fertilized developing egg embryo that is boiled and eaten from the shell.

∞

"You're going to the Philippines for college." Those were the words that would change my life forever. Before I start this story, you need to know a few key things.

1. This story spans five years of my time in my hometown, Baguio.

2. There is an actual story of the time I spent there that I have been writing for years.

3. This story is about *Lolo*.

It was the first day of my freshman year at the University. I had a 7 AM class and my alarms made sure that I'd leave my house an hour early. The morning? Hated it. *How did I do this every day in high school?* The cold air hugged me and made me shiver. I was an island boy; the cold and I weren't exactly friends.

But I wore shorts anyway. I would need to walk through the neighborhood, pass the basketball court, and walk painfully up a hill just to grab a taxi and get to school. Commuting was big there; it's practically how anyone got anywhere. Literally, no excuses. On that short walk to the taxi area, I would encounter the sweetest grandpa. He always greeted, "Good morning" every day as he stood at the same spot near the bakery. His smile was so inviting.

He never once hovered every time we had our brief encounters. He always carried a bag of freshly baked *pandesal* with him. I knew they were fresh because of the sweet aroma of the baked dough that made its way into my nose when he would wave. And every single time, I would deny his offer of one.

Two months would have passed since I left Guam and became an English Literature student. I hated every moment of it. I had other plans on the mainland, but I was stuck in the Philippines. At least, I got to see *Lolo* every morning. The short routine of exchanges with the elder I didn't know anything about somehow made the start of my day a great one. There were days I could get a few sentences in exchange with him, but it was tough. He didn't know any spec of English, and my Tagalog wasn't very good, non-existent really.

But he'd still offer me a piece of *pandesal* every time. As time passed, my brief encounters with *Lolo* became lesser than usual. Around my second year of college, I would get dropped off at school by my uncle most of the time, and when we passed by the bakery, there he was, at the same spot with the bag of bread in his hands. I didn't realize how this *Lolo* had a significant impact on me until his greetings suddenly stopped. On the first week of my Senior year, *Lolo* was nowhere to be found. I froze in my trails that day.

For the first time in four years, I took a moment to look around my surroundings. I've taken this route to the taxi area for years and hadn't noticed how alive it was. There was a routine here as well, apart from me and *Lolo's* greetings to one another. I heard a *walis tingting* being used, the ringing of the bells when the ice cream man made his run through the neighborhood. The *taho* and *balut* individuals challenged each other on who could announce their arrival the loudest, and of course, the smell of *pandesal* getting baked to perfection. I heard, smelt, and saw many things that day but not a sight of *Lolo. Maybe he's not feeling good?*

But that went on for the next few weeks, then months. And every day, I caught myself waiting longer and longer for him, hoping he would approach me with his big smile. Eventually, I'd long for his offer of *pandesal*.

One day, I had it. I approached the bakery owner, stood where *Lolo* would typically be, and asked, "*Kuya*, what happened to the *Lolo* that would buy *pandesal* every morning?"

"Oh... he died, *Ading*." The bakery man uttered.

No...

When the owner's words entered my ears, my heart sank as if a flood of sorrow filled my chest, ready to pour out. I stood there trying to process those words, and before I knew it, I was bawling my eyes out in front of *Kuya*. That feeling was similar to when I had lost my grandpa. I wanted to tell *Lolo* everything, I should have told him everything.

I wanted to tell him I made lots of friends and started dancing again when I thought I had given up on it. I wanted to talk to him about this girl I started to like or share with him what I learned in my Filipino classes. I just wanted to talk to him. But I never got *Lolo's* name, we never had a proper conversation, and I'll never get to accept his offer for pandesal. He will never know he was a friend to me.

"He said to give you this if you ever come asking for him. It's already been paid." The baker handed me a bag of *pandesa*l. I opened it and the sweet scent took me back to when I first waved at *Lolo*. I grabbed one and let it sit on my palm, warm and soft like a child held my hand. One big bite was all it took. I shook my head with a soft grin; I could see why he smiled every morning.

THE BOY AND HIS TEAPOT

Hello!

The God of Tea told us that our sole purpose as teapots will be to heal our owner and whomever they share us with. All I ever wanted was to be needed. We do not choose our bodies; we are gifted them. When a teapot is made, we will be tugged from the haven we first call home. I waited a long time. But it was worth it. I was pulled. As I descended to my new form, I sensed that my creator poured all the love they had into molding me. I am a marbled jade teapot.

Not too flashy, but strong. That same day, I met my owner. His face pouted as he pulled me out of the box, not something a ten-year-old was expecting as a gift. As he held me up, I sensed his heart was mighty. He was not pleased with me for quite some time, but I was determined to brew the mightiest of teas for him.

For five months I would not be used, but that didn't matter. I knew eventually, my time would come. And so, it did. He came home from school, soaked from the rain, and within hours, was hacking up a storm. My little boy needed me, but I knew my plea could not be heard. Luckily, his Mum was there and filled me up with brimming Jade tea. I did what I knew best and brewed all the herbs together and mixed them with my love. Just one sip was all he needed, and his heart would become mighty again.

From that moment, my little boy made it a habit to brew Jade tea every morning before he left for school. And every tea I made was boiled so delicately, he would never be sick again. I made sure of it. Several weeks passed, then months, and years. My little boy wasn't so little anymore. He brought a young lady home, for whom his mighty heart pounded so loudly. She had kind eyes, and her laugh brightened his face. That was the day I no longer brewed just for him.

"Tea?" Her eyebrows curved.

"Yes." My boy chuckled. "You said you weren't feeling good today." He sat teacups next to me.

"It was more on how I'm feeling, Sage. Not physically." She smiled.

"What's the difference?" My boy tilted his head. Yes, what is the difference?

"Hmm? You have a point."

"Well, this will cure you. I've been drinking it for years now and I've never gotten sick." He smiled and reassured her.

"Really? Must be magic tea then?" She picked up a cup and cupped it with her hands.

He poured for her his favorite tea that I have made hundreds of times. I was a bit nervous she would not like my tea but as she sipped, her cheeks lifted, and then she gulped it down. I was relieved. That day, I was almost out of tea, but I felt full. His eighteenth birthday was the day he took it a step further and decided to share me with his family and friends. If I had a heart, it would have been roaring. As he made sure, I was present for birthdays, holidays, celebrations, and the day my little boy would become a father.

That was years ago, so much has changed. My not-so-little boy left home and built a life with his family. I stayed with Mum. Though I still make the best tea that my family believes I do, it's been a while since I brewed anything. Having my boy home is a gift, and I will wait patiently for his visit. But... how many times has he gotten ill because I could not protect him?

Oh... this is what I worry about, but I have poured him years of love, it should protect him for a long time.

I worry for Mum, too. She's been inside her room for days. I want to make her the same tea she made for my little boy when he was sick. I can protect her too. The door creaks open. If I had legs, I'd be jumping right now. She looks a bit different.

I think she got a new haircut, it's way shorter than what she normally had. Please, Mum, let me make you some tea. She stands by the sink, pouring water into a cup from the faucet. She looks at my cabinet's direction and lingers her stare. Yes, Mum! Let me heal you. She walks over and pulls me out, placing me on the table.

I can almost feel the excitement. But she stands still, her back facing me. Mum? She turns my way, If I could smile, I'd be doing it. She takes a deep breath and wobbles in my direction, reaching for me. Her fingers touch me, but they do not grab me. I am pushed and before I know it, I'm on the floor with Mum.

I was right, I am a strong teapot. I did not break. Mum stares at me. She's not moving. Mum? I don't see the light in her eyes anymore. Mum?

I'm Here

My boy places me on the fire. I know this tea by heart. He sits at the table, and I do what I do best, boiling all the herbs to make the magic tea as he calls it.

"Mum..." His voice cracks. He leans his elbows on the table and pours out heavy water from his eyes. Do not be sad, my boy. Mum is not gone; she is at her haven. She will see you again. But he keeps on pouring. His heart is no longer mighty.

I just want to hug him. I want to tell him, I'm here. But, what am I feeling? How can I feel? All I want to do is heal him. But why can't he hear me? Sage! I'm here! Nothing, he hears nothing. I'm here... my boy. He needs my tea. I brew, I boil, and I whistle.

He looks up, wiping his eyes, and turns off the fire. He brings me to the table and takes a teacup. This is the only way I can tell him, tell him how much I care about him. He pours my love and I remember the first time he sipped. He closes his eyes and mimics my memory. And there it is, a smile appears on his face. Welcome home, my boy.

∞

My Boy

The house does not feel so big anymore. My boy has come back with his family. Bigger than I remember. Three little boys are running around, each resembling my boy at different stages in his life. The woman for whom his heart beats loudly stays home with me, she and I make lots of tea together. She reminds me a lot of Mum.

"Honey, I'm home." My boy announces.

"Daddy!" His youngest one jumps in his arms.

"Hey, Dad." The eldest one waves.

"Drew, you're on break from the Uni?" My boy drops his youngest and hugs his eldest.

"Term break just started."

"We have you for a week? Thank the heavens." My boy looks up. It's a good day for tea. My boy's lady turns the fire on, and they all sit at the table, starting supper. I brew the finest tea in the world, only the best for my family. My boy tells his middle son to fetch me as I whistle in completion. This boy is much softer, he's a lot like my boy. He lifts me gently and walks us over to the family. This feels... familiar. A good familiar. As the middle son pours, his finger slips and touches my heated bottom.

I feel the wind inside me. I had only ever felt it once before I was made into a teapot, waiting up in the clouds to be pulled down to my body. As my tea lay on the floor, and pieces of me scattered around, I see my little boy looking at me for the first time. He's become such a beautiful man. He hovers over me, with water pouring from his eyes, just like he did with Mum.

I don't want to go... I want to stay... but I broke. I must leave now... oh, my boy... how I wish I could have healed you for a very long time.

PIN BOY

∞

12:30 AM

"Help!" I scream, my voice reverberating through the house. Hissing and growling, they crawl within the walls like unearthly creatures. Heart racing, I sprint through the black-lit home, footsteps echoing. Palms sweaty, all doors are locked—no escape tonight. "Someone, please help!" I yell, but Thunder drowns my plea. Darkness envelops me. "Leave me alone," I sob, collapsing to my knees.

Claws click on wooden boards, drawing nearer, surrounding me. The creatures are poised. I scream.

∞

Yesterday

11:58 AM

I consider myself an average student, well, in a certain sense. As the dance team captain, I managed to make the head cheerleader my girlfriend and climb the social ladder in the popular crowd. With graduation looming, success seemed within reach. However, that morning, something shifted. It was Senior Prank Day, and my best friend Dexter had a plan.

"What the fuck, man? This is the dumbest fucking idea you've ever come up with. Stop this shit right now!" I warned Dexter in a low voice so no one would hear.

"Dude, what the fuck's been up with you? Who the hell cares about Pin Boy?

"What did Carlos ever do to you anyway?"

"He's just so fucking weird; ever since we were kids, he had those fucking stupid clothespins with him every day like they're fucking action figures. Who the fuck does that?"

"And then? Who fucking cares what he does with his time?"

"His face just fucking irritates me," Dexter admitted with pride.

"We were all close at one point," I said softly.

"In elementary, Bon. That was ancient fucking history."

"You don't think having the whole senior class targeting just him isn't taking it too far?"

"Bon, do you hear yourself? It's fucking harmless. We're not killing the guy; I just wanna remind him."

"Remind him of what? That he's a loser?"

"Exactly. See, you get it." He smacked my shoulder and smiled.

"No, Dex. I don't get it. What are you, fucking twelve?"

"God, when did you become such a fucking narc. If you don't wanna be a part of it, then just fuck off, Bon."

"Imma just say this one time." I shoved him against the lockers, the bang echoed through the hall. "I'll put you in your fucking place if you mess with him." My arm was pushed against his chest. I didn't know what had gotten into me, but I wouldn't let him go after Carlos.

"Some bold ass threats coming from a guy who's never fought in his life," Dexter snickered. He lunged his chest forward and pushed me off him. "What are you gonna fucking do, huh, Bon? I mean, like anyone will fucking listen to you." He snickered again, but this time Dexter looked at me with disgust like he always did at Carlos. "You got about ten minutes; we'll be there in fifteen. Better start fucking running, hero." Dexter grinned, patting my cheek like I was a pet.

Fuck! I started running through the hallway. How have I never seen this before? My nails dig into my palms. My whole life I've been so fucking blind. My breath comes in short little gasps as I race down the stairs. My best friend's a goddamn bully. Visions swim through my head. That time with Kurt. And last year with Jessica. And little Mindy. I shake my head but there's more and more floating to the surface. Dexter's been terrorizing kids all his life. And I just let it happen.

"Woah!" I slammed into someone coming from around the corner. "I'm sor—Babe?" I let out while panting.

"Where the heck are you going to be running like that?" Aiesha giggled and moved her hair out of her face.

"I'm sorry, baby, I need to stop Dexter." I tried to catch my breath and leaned against the wall.

"I seriously hate your best friend." She rubbed my back.

"Same,"

"Wait." Aiesha furrowed at me. "Did I hear this right? You just said something bad about Dexter? The guy who can do no wrong in your eyes?" She crossed her arms and looked at me like I was a different person.

"Yeah, he's an asshole. I should have listened to you."

"Finally!" She jumped at me for a hug, and I caught her, almost missing. "You need to start picking your friends, baby. That boy is a wolf in sheep's clothing." She kissed me on the cheek.

"I can't let them do that to Carlos."

"Then don't." Aiesha pulled away from our embrace. "What are you gonna do to stop it?"

I can't help but feel like I was a kid again and I didn't say anything to defend Carlos from Dexter. I regretted it for so long, maybe I can make it up to him now. "I could... I could get to Carlos first. Get him out of there before they start."

"There you go. I can get the team to try and stop some of the seniors." Aiesha nodded.

"Really?"

"Yes, now go!"

I started running toward the courtyard but stopped in my tracks, turning back around. There she still was, smiling at me. For the first time, I realized how much I loved Aisha. I ran back to her and locked my lips with hers. "I love you," I said after our kiss, not realizing I had uttered those three words.

"I love you too, now go!" Aiesha pointed to the courtyard, and I was off.

The courtyard was on the other side of the campus. No matter how quickly I hustled, time felt like it was on fast-forward. Couldn't shake Carlos from my thoughts. He was always the quiet type, and that didn't do him any favors when he crossed paths with Dexter. Our trio split in sixth grade when Carlos opted out of joining sports with us, navigating middle and high school solo. But, even then, he always had those four clothespins by his side.

"Carlos!" I yelled, spotting him at the table, but my shouts were lost in the distance. "Car—" I cut off as a crowd surged toward him. "Damn it." Dodging through the crowd, I noticed the water balloons in their hands. A broad circle formed around him. Oblivious, Carlos wore his hood, head down, engrossed in playing with his pins.

I broke out of the crowd, about to scream for him when Dexter and the football team arrived. Dexter locked eyes with me and gave me the same smug smirk he always had.

"Carlos!" I shouted, and Carlos picked his head up, confused to see everyone.

"Now!" Dexter yelled, hurling the first water balloon at Carlos's face. Laughter and screams filled the air as everyone joined in the water balloon onslaught. All I could do was watch as the barrage soaked Carlos. Dexter glared at me, and I shot him a defiant look, catching the water balloon he tossed my way. I wouldn't play his games any longer.

Raising the water balloon to my face, I burst it. The onslaught finally ceased, and Carlos knelt with his hood off, drenched. Dexter approached him, mockingly clapping. "Pin boy! Congrats! You're now officially the school joke," Dexter taunted, igniting laughter.

Carlos lifted his head, scanning the area until his eyes landed on me.

"Right, Bon?" Dexter turned to me, and everyone's attention shifted. The pressure mounted, thoughts racing in my head about my reputation and the choices ahead. A tug-of-war between preserving my image and standing up for an old friend.

Under the weight of the moment, I caved. "Freak." Silence lingered, Dexter, grinning in triumph. In my eyes, Carlos would see only the fear of my choice. "Look at Pin Boy, can't even tell if he's crying," I teased, prompting laughter.

"Let's go, y'all. Let Pin Boy dry out in the sun," Dexter said, leading the way. The crowd dispersed, leaving Carlos alone. Heartbroken, I locked eyes with him, his head bowed, water dripping. As I turned away, shattered by my actions, Aiesha appeared with tears in her eyes. She shook her head and ran away.

"Aiesha, wait!" I called, sprinting after her. Glancing back at Carlos, his eyes were watery. I caught up to Aiesha, grabbing her waist.

"You monster!" she yelled. "Get off of me!"

I released her, tears welling up. "I'm letting you go; I'm letting you go."

"How could you do that to him?" Aiesha gripped my shirt.

"I know, I know," I cried. "I was going to stop Dex, but everyone looked at me, and all I could hear was me being a failure if I didn't do what Dex expected."

"Is popularity that important to you?"

"No... Yes? I- I don't know! I will fix this; I'll make it up to Carlos tomorrow and tell the principal that Dexter planned it all. I'll take responsibility. I promise."

"Tell that to Carlos; you hurt him." Aiesha walked away.

Nothing stings more than seeing Aiesha hurt. Though I yearned to chase after her, I knew what needed to be done. Heading to the principal's office, I spilled everything. My reputation wasn't worth losing Aiesha and hurting Carlos. How did I let myself become a bully? My honesty granted me forgiveness from the principal. The penalty for bullying Carlos was a five-day suspension, absent from my school record. In contrast, Dexter faced a twenty-day suspension and expulsion from the football team.

Aiesha texted, asking for a few days to collect herself. I respected her choice; I'd hate myself too. After the principal informed my parents and clarified the situation, they sent me home. Parking my car in the driveway, I headed straight upstairs to shower. Carlos' sad face and the water dripping off him played on a loop in my mind. After putting on shorts and a T-shirt, the softness of the bed eased my body, and I found myself drifting.

The enticing scent of Mom's cooking roused me from my nap; it had been longer than I realized. Descending the stairs, I entered the kitchen.

"Sit down, honey; we're just about to start," Mom said, arranging the table.

"How's practice going?" Dad asked casually as if they hadn't received a call about my suspension.

"Great, Dad. Coach has been praising me more each day," I replied casually.

"That's good! Work your way for that scholarship," he beamed. "I know you're suspended right now, and I generally would be mad, but you tried to stop Dexter. And this whole thing isn't going on your record, so your shot at that scholarship isn't jeopardized. That's all that matters."

I gazed at him, wanting to express my true feelings, that a scholarship was the last thing on my mind. But all I managed was a soft smile.

"Honey, please bless the food," Mom urged, taking her seat and looking at Dad.

He nodded and began, "Amen, let's eat."

"Amen," Mom and I echoed in unison.

This was my favorite part of the day, engaging in family conversation around the table while the aroma of Mom's cooking enveloped the house. It was the only time I could let my guard down. Aiesha's words echoed in my head, "You monster!" The phone rang, and Mom rose to answer it, giving Dad an opening to talk about dance with me.

Yet, my thoughts drifted back to the earlier fiasco at school, wishing I had stood up to Dexter as planned. Mom hung up the phone and slowly returned to the table, her distressed expression catching Dad's attention.

"Honey, what's wrong?" Dad asked.

"Bonnin... I don't..." Her voice started to crack.

"Honey, what is it?"

Mom's breathing quickened. "Carlos..."

"What?" I snapped out of my thoughts, having missed her words.

Mom wiped her tears.

"Oh, my god..." Dad's face turned pale.

What did Mom say again? Silence settled, the atmosphere somber. It felt like someone had just passed away, probably a relative. I wanted to ask what happened, but I had no energy to talk.

"I'm tired." I set my utensils on my plate. "I'm going to bed; thanks for the food, Mom." I stood up.

"Oh, my baby..." Mom embraced me tightly.

I raised a brow.

Dad nodded, not looking up at me.

I made my way to the stairs and glanced back. Dad was comforting Mom. I hesitated. Should I go back? Shaking my head, I headed for my room. The door rattled as I slammed it shut and fell onto my bed. My hand reached for my phone on my left, and I began checking my social media.

My hands shook as I scrolled through my timeline. "RIP Carlos?" I said, confused. My eyes widened, and my heart grew heavy. "Carlos..." I sat up. Why are they all saying this?

I realized Mom and Dad had told me, but I ignored the entire conversation, much like I had ignored Carlos' plea for help. Anger surged within me; all the people posting about Carlos were the reason he was gone. In a fit of rage, I texted Dexter:

Murderer

I powered down my phone, slipped under the blankets, and shielded my head with a pillow.

12:23 AM

The sound of thunder jolts me awake. I reach for my phone, checking the time amid another roar. Feeling uneasy, I leave my room to find Mom and Dad. No response as I call out on the way down. In the kitchen, I discover a note on the fridge: "Helping the Gallaways, back late. Mom and Dad," it reads.

Thunder and lightning synchronize, startling me. Simultaneously, the power blacks out. "Great," I mutter. Activating my phone's flashlight, I ascend the stairs when abrupt footsteps scurry on the second floor. Pausing, I aim my phone at the noise, revealing nothing. Then, a loud bang echoes from the walls near the stairs.

I press my ear against the wall, feeling its chill. Another thud startles me. It's like something's scurrying in the walls, crawling up the stairs. Stunned, I cautiously ascend. Then my phone dies, and I gasp. Panicking, I dash to my parent's room, locking the door. *Where's the fucking flashlight? The closet!* Dad has a portable lamp in there.

Digging through the closet, I spot the lamp up high by the shoe boxes. I flick it on, pointing it at the door. Outside, I hear rustling. It stops. A baseball bat catches my eye, and I snatch it. Opening the door slowly, I peek out, take a deep breath, and then burst into the hallway, bat raised.

Glancing around, I shout, "I gotta fucking bat! Show yourself!" Lightning strikes, revealing a silhouette in front of me.

Sprinting to my room, I search for my old phone, hoping it still functions. As I enter, I hear scuttling sounds. Raising the lamp, I approach the bookshelf. Something moves, and as I get closer, I spot a clothespin. To my surprise, it turns, hissing with sharp teeth and fangs. My eyes widen in disbelief.

More hisses echo in the room, and I illuminate it with my lamp. Three additional clothespins fixate on me. They hiss, screech, sprouting wings and displaying slimy teeth. I scream, letting go of the lamp and bat.

"Help!" I scream, my voice reverberating through the house. Hissing and growling, they crawl within the walls like unearthly creatures. Heart racing, I sprint through the black-lit home, footsteps echoing. Palms sweaty, all doors are locked—no escape tonight. "Someone, please help!" I yell, but Thunder drowns my plea. Darkness envelops me. "Leave me alone," I sob, collapsing to my knees.

Claws click on wooden boards, drawing nearer, surrounding me. The creatures are poised. I scream. The pins encircle me, jaws filled with doom. Hissing stops as they lower to the floor, attention shifting to the stairs. Heavy footsteps ascend. My heart pounds; the alpha is near.

The footsteps approach, and I glimpse a figure. No, it's... my eyes widen in horror. "Carlos?" I stammer. Carlos lunges at me. The pins hiss and screech, seemingly cheering for their meal. He shrieks, grabbing my neck. My eyes open, gasping.

Heart racing, palms sweaty, I catch my breath, clutching my neck. The choking sensation lingers. Checking my phone, the truth hits me. "Carlos is really gone," my voice trembles. A memory surfaces, prompting me to get out of bed. I search beneath, finding a dusty old box. Opening it reveals the clothespins.

"Are those clothespins?"

"They are, but check this; they look like little monsters, right?" I smile, holding up one.

"Yeah. They could even have wings to be scarier."

"Exactly. And they can even have slimy teeth. I'm Bonnin."

"I'm Carlos," he smiles.

"Here, take four of my pins so you can make them whatever you want," I offer.

The memory overwhelms me. "Carlos, I'm so sorry," I cry over the box filled with pins and a picture of us when we were young.

THE WITCH OF ALBATROSS

HER STORY HAS JUST BEGUN

Run, Witch, Run!

In the distant past, a young girl named Esmeralda resided in the quiet town of Albatross. Adored by many, she was destined to inherit her family's business. However, as Esmeralda matured, her uniqueness became apparent. Ahead of her time, she concocted herbs and remedies at the age of eight and devoured most of the books in her town's library. Occasionally, townsfolk witnessed her conversing with animals. By eighteen, Esmeralda was feared, particularly by men who accused her of witchcraft.

On the flip side, the women reveled in Esmeralda's gifts. They sought her guidance for matters of marriage or asked questions that only revealed truths to her. While she was content to help people, her parents became wary, influenced by the news of the Salem trials. They feared their daughter might face persecution from the town due to her abilities. On her nineteenth birthday, the town, armed with pitchforks and torches, marched to her house. They aimed to make Esmeralda suffer at the stake, but with her loving parents' assistance, she narrowly escaped into the woods. Sprinting deep into the forest and up a cliff, the sight of her home consumed by flames left her in shock.

Her cries of despair reverberated through the forest as she wept.

"Are you lost?" inquired a gentle child's voice.

Esmeralda, startled, turned around, wiping her tears, but there was no one in sight.

"Over here."

Looking up, she spotted a white owl. "Hello," Esmeralda greeted it.

"Are you lost?" the owl tilted its head.

"Yes, I don't have anywhere to go." She extended her hand, and the owl perched on it.

"My master is not far from here. Do you wish to come with me?"

"Yes, anywhere but here." Esmeralda raised her arm, and the owl soared.

She followed the owl deeper into the forest, the smoke from her home now visible high in the sky. Thoughts of her family and hopes for their escape occupied her mind. A bright orange light ahead diverted Esmeralda's attention. To her surprise, three young girls, around nine or ten, sat around a bonfire. The owl descended, landing on a lady's arm—his master. In that moment, the lady locked eyes with her and offered the most welcoming smile.

"What's your name, darling?" inquired the lady.

"Esmeralda." Her voice trembled.

"My name is Gilda. Where are you from, Esmeralda?"

"Albatross, ma'am." She shivered from the cold.

"Oh, my dear, look at you." Gilda walked toward her, wrapping her in a blanket. "What happened?"

"The town came for me in anger... My parents had me escape just in time..." Esmeralda's recollection stirred a torrent of emotions, overwhelming her. She began to sob and sank to her knees. "Everything happened so quickly. I... I didn't have a chance to say goodbye to my family."

The three little girls approached Esmeralda and enveloped her in embraces.

The eldest girl pulled away, saying, "I'm Kelsey, and this is my little sister Anya and my cousin Joy."

Anya and Joy greeted Esmeralda, clinging to her arms.

"My mommy was hung in front of me," Joy's voice cracked.

Esmeralda's chest sank. She couldn't fathom witnessing her mother's death, let alone at Joy's age.

"Our mommy tried to help Aunt Lily, but she..." Anya couldn't finish her sentence.

"They burned her alive and let the people watch while they cheered," Kelsey hugged her little sister. "We were next, but our dads told us to just keep running into the forest. Then we met Miss Gilda."

Esmeralda's heart ached for them. She grappled with conflicting emotions, unsure whether to feel guilty for knowing her family could have escaped while these little girls' families couldn't.

"Do you know why they came for you? All of you?" Gilda questioned the girls.

No one had the answer; fear held them in its grip.

"You are witches. We all are."

The girls exchanged glances.

"A witch? No." Esmeralda shook her head.

"Are there things you could do that you cannot explain?" Gilda probed.

This question stirred something in each of the girls. Though they could have answered Gilda, fear silenced them.

"Kelsey, Anya, Joy, can either of you speak to my owl?"

The three little girls shook their heads.

"But you can, Esmeralda."

Esmeralda remained silent; she couldn't deny it. She had known since she was a young girl that she was different from everyone in her town.

"Don't be afraid. What people have said about witches is nothing but fear of what they cannot understand," Gilda knelt to them. "We are everything they are and so much more. We are sisters now, and we must protect each other." Gilda affirmed and embraced them.

A sense of comfort enveloped the girls. Esmeralda felt the same warmth she had with her family. For now, she had her newfound sisters, and all she could think of was survival.

∞

As The Story Goes

Years passed, and Esmeralda made the decision to part ways with her Coven. The witch hunt had faded, and she felt a sudden urge to return to Albatross. Her sisters were supportive of her decision, wishing her safe travels. However, the most challenging goodbyes were to Kelsey, Anya, and Joy, who now had families of their own.

"Esme, my big sister, please protect yourself by any means necessary." Kelsey embraced her tightly.

"I learned all my protective spells from you, Kels. They better watch out." Esmeralda tightened her embrace.

"I want a hug too, Big Sis." Anya leaped into Esmeralda's arms and sobbed. "I love you, please return."

"Thank you, Little Sis. I promise to return. I'll always be nearby; just look up at the stars."

"I hope you find what you're looking for." Joy's voice cracked as she cradled her newborn.

"Thank you, Little One." Esmeralda walked over to Joy and kissed her forehead.

Joy tried holding back her tears, but as strong as she let herself be, her tears flowed down her cheeks.

"Come back home to us." Joy sobbed.

Kelsey and Anya joined to embrace their sisters.

"Gilda would be proud," Kelsey told Esmeralda.

"She'd be proud of all of us," Esmeralda reassured them all. "You too, Charlie."

The white owl circled over them. Charlie had become Esmeralda's familiar after Gilda passed. Gilda's words echoed in Esmeralda's thoughts. 'A bond between a witch and their familiar is like no other; it's as if your souls are intertwined.'

"Take care of the Coven," Esmeralda requested the girls.

That was the only thing Esmeralda asked before embarking on her and Charlie's grand journey back to where it all began. Several fortnights passed, and she finally reached the cliff. After all these years, Esmeralda returned home. Her memories of her hometown were tainted by fear, but her love for her family and the hope she held onto outweighed anything and kept her alive. Staring from a distance, it appeared that the town had not changed. It was the same as when she left it. "Please, Ma and Pa, I'm home, find me."

Only if they could feel her heart and how much it ached for them.

She stayed by the cliff, keeping her distance far enough not to be noticed. Esmeralda was a Nature Witch, a proud one too. She created a small hut by conjuring vines from the ground and knitted them together to make Charlie's and her new home. She sprinkled magic-induced powder around the hut and instantly grew colorful flowers. She cast a spell on the flowers to make her home invisible to anyone. On most days, Esmeralda stood on the cliff where she saw her home burnt to a crisp, hovering over the town, crying and hoping to see her parents once more.

But as days turned to weeks and months turned to years, Esmeralda accepted that her family was no longer around.

One day, a shriek of helplessness from a young lady caught Esmeralda's attention.

"You're not going to help her?" Charlie scorned Esmeralda.

"It's people like her who cast me away. Why should I help?" She ignored the cries.

"Someone please, help!" The young lady shouted and fell to the ground. "He's not going to make it, please..." The lady sobbed.

"Esmeralda, please, look at her. You're not a monster," Charlie said. "Doesn't this look familiar?"

As much as Esmeralda hated to admit it, Charlie was right. The young lady reminded Esmeralda of the day she lost her family. Helpless, scared, and lost, then came Charlie, who saved her.

"Where is he?" Esmeralda extended her hand to the disheveled girl on the ground.

She looked up and reached for Esmeralda's hand.

"Right this way," the young lady exclaimed.

She led Esmeralda to the young boy, and instantly, Esmeralda's eyes widened. His bones protruded out of his body, and his limbs were twisted.

"He fell off the tree. He wanted to pick the fruits for me. I tried telling him it was too dangerous, but he wouldn't listen! He's so stubborn!"

Esmeralda examined the boy and saw that he was still breathing. The young lady shrieked, and Esmeralda turned to her, spotting a grizzly bear approaching them.

"I need your help," Esmeralda commanded the beast.

The bear stood on its two legs and growled.

"Fine, a jar of honey it is," Esmeralda negotiated. "Carry him and follow me."

The bear walked over to the boy and carried him like a baby.

"Hey!" The young lady shouted at the bear.

"Don't worry. He's safe. Follow me," Esmeralda instructed her.

They all rushed to her hut. With a clap of her hands, the flowers floated, and the spell was lifted, revealing her home.

The young lady gasped, "You're a witch... Please save my Bobby." The young lady pleaded. Esmeralda told her to move back and called out to her animal friends. A cluster of spiders appeared and began cocooning Bobby.

"What are they doing?" The young lady shuddered.

"Saving his life."

Esmeralda walked over to Bobby's body and helped the spiders web him. Charlie swooped in and grabbed some of the webs with his talons, making sure every part of his body was covered. The spiders dispersed. Esmeralda then called upon the young lady.

"What is your name, darling?"

"Annie."

"All right, Annie. This part is very important," Esmeralda placed both their hands on the cocooned Bobby's chest. "Think of a memory you and Bobby shared and think of how much you love him."

Annie shut her eyes tightly. As Annie did her part of the spell, Esmeralda recited an incantation repeatedly until the webs began to deteriorate. Esmeralda smiled. The spell worked. Bobby woke up, and all his injuries had been cured. Annie wept in joy and thanked Esmeralda profusely. Bobby thanked her as well and had no memory of anything that just unfolded.

"Annie, that spell only worked because of you. You helped me cast it.

You're a witch." Esmeralda embraced her.

Annie was too baffled to react to the information.

"Don't worry, you won't have to practice. Just live your life."

Esmeralda scooped up some powder from her pouch and blew a memory spell on them to forget her. Before the couple could react, the spell had been cast, and they instantly forgot why they were there in the first place. Esmeralda stared at them from her home, invisible to anyone. Something happened to Esmeralda that day because she made a vow to protect the town that shunned her. From then on, every full blue moon of the year, she placed a spell on the town for protection.

To this day, flowers grow deep in the woods. Some say it's Esmeralda, who still waits for her parents to come and find her.

FROM ME

Six months. It took six long, excruciating months to get myself back on my feet. I gaze into the mirror for the first time since the breakup, and in utter horror, my beard has reached its hobo peak. My hair is shoulder length, resembling the Asian equivalent of Jesus; funny enough, I was never religious. I inhale deeply and exhale a big sigh. What have I done to myself? I don't even recognize the person staring back at me right now.

∞

HAIRCUT

I grab my keys without hesitation and make for the barbershop.

The drive isn't that long from my apartment but the outside is definitely a refreshing scenery. I enter the shop, and the bells ring, announcing my arrival. Sam, my barber, turns his head and beams a huge smile toward me.

"You're back." He says earnestly.

I smile, and he ushers me to the seat. *Am I next already?*

"It's been a while." He pats my shoulders.

I sit.

We both stare at the mirror.

"We've got some work." He says with a smile, and I take no offense.

"Yeah, been a rough time." I nonchalantly joke.

"No need to explain, that's why I'm here. I got you." He squeezes my shoulder.

"Thank you, Sam." I smile. *How could I let myself get like this?*

∞

"Wake up, sleepy head." Sam nudges me, and I sit up straight.

Shit, I dozed off. I guess staying in and sleeping for most days, made me physically tired. Mentally? I was already there way before the breakup.

"What do you think?" He smiles, proud of his creation. As he should be. My hair is cut shorter than usual, with a fade on both sides. My beard is trimmed and looking clean. He managed to make me look not as depressed as I am.

I give a soft smile, approving.

"Alright, let's get you washed up."

I get up and follow him to the hairwasher. The cold water contacts my scalp and his fingers run through my hair. The smell of cotton candy enters my nose as he massages my head with the shampoo. Could this be the defining moment? Washing off all the hurt I feel. Only if it was that simple. I wish it was that simple. We return to the seat, and he dries my hair with a hair blower. Wow, I transformed from Asian Jesus to Thor, God of Thunder. Haircuts, man, they really do wonders. Sam makes some final touches and massages my back and head; this is going to make me fall asleep again. Barbers don't get enough credit. What they can do with hair is pure magic.

"Look at that." He leans to my right, "Haircuts aren't just for show; there is a lot of power in changing how people see us." He smiles. "Looking good, brotha." He takes off the apron covering my body.

I pull out my wallet, but he shakes his head.

"On me." I get taken aback by his gesture.

"Sam, take my money."

"Just make sure to take care of yourself, okay?" He smiles at me as the next customer sits on the chair.

I thank him once more and bid him goodbye. I walk out of the shop, feeling as if I can finally start again. In that instance, a gust of wind blows right through me. The winds of change?

Friends

It's Friday night. I know exactly where the Originals are going to be. The Originals became our group name not because we love the Vampire Diaries, but because we've all been friends since middle school. Some of us go even way back to elementary, with twenty years of friendship. I haven't had a night out in months, let alone seen the squad. I have this really bad habit of pushing people away when I go through episodes, so going out of my way to surprise them would be the right thing. Even just being there would do because they've always been there for me. With that in mind, dressing up and looking presentable isn't quite going well for me.

I finally take a proper shower, the cold water cleansing all the bad energies that lingered after the barbershop.

My closet started piling up on my bed while I rummage for an outfit. After thirty minutes of standing naked, I finally decided on a fit, a black T-shirt with maroon shorts. I'm basic as hell. I dust the lint off my clothes, staring at the mirror once more before leaving my bat cave. The pomade Kelsey got me last year still works. Out of nowhere, a tear sneaks out of my left eye, taking me by surprise. *No.*

"You're gonna be okay," I tell myself and put on my biggest smile.

I lock the door and head to my car. 10:15 PM. They should be drunk by now. I miss them a lot. They've been supportive and respectful during all of this; coming out and seeing their faces is what I need right now. It has to be. I get to the club and parked Appa, my beat-up 2010 SUV.

I check their IG stories, and they're about three shots in. I get out of the car, hesitant, but I make my way to the entrance. I can feel the bass of the music intensifying as I approach the door. The bouncer checks my ID and lets me in. I soak it all up; I haven't had human contact in months, and here I am surrounded by strangers grinding on each other. My face lights up. It doesn't take long for me to spot Chanse, Celeste, Aura, Sunshine, and Antonia in the middle of the club around a table. The neon lights flicker and blind me for a moment.

"He's out!" Celeste shouts, and the group runs toward me.

They all take turns hugging me. I'm so deprived of love.

"I can't believe you're out!" Chanse yells over the music.

"I miss you guys!" I say earnestly.

Celeste gives me a shot glass and passes one to everybody at the table. "To Sky, we love you, bitch!" She screams.

"Sky!" Everyone shouts in unison, and we tilt our heads back.

The liquor burns my throat, and I feel a sting on my chest.

"How's your arm?" Sunshine slightly grips my hand.

"It's okay?" I furrow and look at my arm.

Sunshine tilts her head.

I fill up another shot glass and chug it down. I fill up another and retake it, my body numbs and the heat takes over.

"Sky, slow down," Sunshine grabs my arm.

"Come on, guys; we're here to have fun, right? I haven't seen you in months." I slur my words. The lights flicker in synchronization with the beats making my vision hazy, and my body becomes light. I'm spiraling. "Let's dance!" I shout.

Everyone glances at each other.

"Come on, guys; I missed all of you," I say with my twisted tongue and droopy eyes.

"Let's go!" Aura shouts, and everyone follows me to the dance floor.

For the first time in six months, I feel almost happy. A crowd begins to form around us. Celeste starts twerking, and Chanse follows. For the rest of the hour, we dance till our legs can't handle it anymore. If I don't catch my breath, I think my heart's going to give out. But as the next song plays, I freeze. The world around me becomes muffled.

I block everything out, but not this song. I look at the floor and close my eyes. This is the song Kelsey and I first danced to. I saw her walking towards me, and she tripped like the klutz she is. And I caught her, like the hero I thought I was. An outpour of memories we had together, years of memories I wish we could build more, enters my heart.

"Sky!" I hear a low voice ringing in my ear.

It was too late; the ache of my soul pours out of my eyes.

"This was their song." I hear Celeste say.

"Dancing Queen?" Antonia questions.

It was. It really felt like ours. I- how did I get here? *How did I let it get this far?*

Chanse hugs me tightly. Celeste follows, and so does everyone. The music thumps my eardrums and everyone in the club dances their hearts out, while my best friends and I embrace in the middle of the club. All our hearts are embracing one another, giving me comfort, and making sure I don't feel alone. I feel alive. I cry, not because of the pain, but for the love that's overpowering me.

"Let's get some fresh air," Chanse yells to everyone. We break our huddle and wipe our tears. We interlock our hands with one another, and Chanse leads the way out of the club. As the doors open, the cool breeze hits every part of my body. I take a deep breath in and exhale.

"I'm sorry, guys," I wipe more of my tears. "I'm sorry I ruined the night."

"No." They all say and surround me with sadness in their eyes.

"Stop being sorry, Sky." Aura pats my back.

"Never be sorry for feeling anything." Chanse rubs my back too.

"Yeah." Everyone agrees.

"I know but, I thought I could do this, come out and just be normal again. I thought I was stronger." My voice cracks.

"Look where you're at now; you came out tonight when you didn't need to. You're strong, Sky; we're so happy you're here." Celeste's voice cracks.

Everyone's eyes fill with tears.

"We love you, Sky." Each of them tells me.

My chest becomes heavy, "I love you guys so much."

They embrace me once again, and this time I feel lighter, not from the alcohol but as if a heavy weight has lifted off my chest. "I wish I got out and saw all of you sooner." I cry into somebody's chest.

"That's okay; we understand," Aura says.

"Take all the time you need; we'll be waiting for you," Antonia said shakily.

"I know." I nod, still sobbing.

"We'll never leave you; you know that, right?" Sunshine assures me.

I pick my head up, and we break from our embrace.

"Fuck," I laugh and wipe my tears. "This breakup hurts more than I thought." I look at all of them and see the same sad-confused expression sitting on their face.

Chanse looks back at Celeste, and they both mouth something to each other.

The soft beats from the club echo.

"Guys?" I say. They stare at me as if they've just seen a ghost.

"What do you mean breakup?" Chanse asks.

"Me and Kelsey... we broke up?"

"Holy shit." Aura lets out and turns away.

"What?" I frown my eyes.

Antonia and Sunshine begin crying.

"Sky... you guys, didn't break up..." Chanse has a hard time speaking.

"What do you mean we didn't break up? She told me she wanted a break." I raise my voice, puffing my chest.

"When did she tell you that?" Celeste furrows.

"When I was dropping her home that night? Why are you guys weird?"

"Because..." Celeste pauses.

"Because... Kelsey's dead, Sky..." Chanse lets out.

I don't say a thing. My head is trying to understand if I heard that right.

"She died that night you gu-"

"Huh?" I cut Chanse off and take a step back. "No, she's not. Why would you say that!"

"I- it's true, Sky. Kelsey's been gone." Aura says looking down.

"No... we- broke up. She said she needed to be alone for a whi—"

The memory comes in fast, and I'm in the car with Kelsey. I'm angry. Both of my hands are gripped tightly on the steering wheel. This was that night.

"You're not listening to me, Sky. That's the one thing you know I hate and you keep doing it! You don't understand what I'm trying to tell you." Kelsey said, facing the window.

"Then let me understand! You want to break up because I don't listen? I'm listening, Kels!"

"That's not the reason! I don't want to break up; I think we need space."

"Why do we need space? We talk it out like how we always do."

"You talk it out. I listen. Because whenever I say anything, you don't get it and it's brushed under the rug. I can't do this anymore."

I turned to her, and I saw it in her eyes, "You don't love me anymore?" I softly let out.

She looked back at me and didn't say a word. A tear escaped my eye and her head turned to the front.

"Sky, look out!" She screamed, and I twisted my head back to the steering wheel and saw a raccoon crossing the road. The car swerved abruptly and before I knew it, we tumbled five times onto a tree.

I drop to the ground, the memory crushing me. "I..." I hold on to my chest, trying to catch my breath. "I fucking killed her."

How did I let it get this far? My eyes open, and the sunlight stings them. I raise my right hand to cover my eyes, peeking through the cracks of my fingers to look at my surroundings. This isn't my house. I'm lying on a couch. My legs are on top of Aura's lap. She's sitting down, sound asleep. Chanse is lying on the floor snoring, while Antonia and Sunshine are cozy up on the bed by the left corner of this apartment studio. Celeste walks out of the shower with a towel on her head, wearing her house clothes. I smile at her, and she goes around to the kitchen and grabs a mug.

I sit up, and Aura turns her back to me, fixing her position. That must've been so uncomfortable. I grab the mug, and the steam of the coffee pelts my nose hairs as I take a whiff of the creamy vanilla.

"Thanks," I say, sipping the hot liquid, feeling the warmth of the caffeine flow down my throat as if cleansing the alcohol in my system. I pull back and blow out the hot air in me.

"Just how you like it, right?" She smiles.

Everyone begins waking up, Chanse the last. Celeste tells me that Aura and Chanse stayed up all night watching over me. They're always taking care of me, all of them. The girls prepare breakfast; Aura falls back asleep, this time taking over the couch. I know she didn't get a good night's rest; she deserves a few more minutes. Chanse and I sit at the dining table and sip our coffee. The girl's cooking envelopes the whole house with the sweet aroma of breakfast sausages and bacon.

"How are you?" Chanse breaks the silence. There are two ways I can interpret this question, how am I from the drinking? Or how am I mentally?

"Okay." I think that's a safe answer.

The food arrives, and Antonia wakes up Aura. We all sit down at the dinner table for breakfast. I check the time, and it's 3:52 PM. I don't mind, I love breakfast food. Celeste leads the prayer. I bow my head for respect, but what can I pray for? Who do I pray for?

"Amen. Let's eat." Celeste smiles, and we start breakfast.

It's silent, all I can hear is the clinging of the utensils on the plate. I catch everyone staring at me before they pull away. I see it in their eyes, how wounded they see me.

"Guys." I break the tension.

Everyone stops chewing and looks at me.

"Don't any of you have work today?"

"We called off," Sunshine answers for everyone.

"This is our first time seeing you in months; we can miss a day of work." Aura softly smiles at me.

I nod slowly, "Also, whose... house are we in?" I take a bite of the sausage.

"Mine, hello." Celeste giggled. "You don't remember my house?" She laughs.

"I don't remember a lot of things," I say without thinking.

It gets quiet again.

"That happens with trauma," Antonia says.

Everyone turns to her.

She stares at her plate, "I read that severe trauma can cause you to forget things. I can see—" She looks up to see everyone staring at her. "Never mind, sorry." She leans back on the chair.

"Antonia's right," I say, and everyone turns to me. "I'll be honest, I really thought we just broke up... I didn't know I was blocking... that out."

"We wish we could have been there for you more," Chanse says.

"You guys were. Really. I mean, I didn't know it was about that, but every one of you always stopped by to make sure I was okay; that helped me a lot."

"But look at you, we thought you were just grieving and..." Celeste stops and drops her utensils on her plate.

"Went crazy." I finish her sentence and giggle.

Everyone stares at me.

"Did— did you guys think I was going to kill myself?" I say bluntly.

"Yes," Chanse admits.

They look astounded that Chanse said anything.

"You disappeared on us. You stopped replying to our calls and messages, and when we would visit you, it was always quiet. We thought you killed yourself, so we called the cops." Chanse takes a deep breath in and exhales.

He must've been holding that in for so long.

"That's why the police came." I lean back on the chair and rub my eyes. "I'm so sorry guys." My voice cracks a little.

"We don't want to lose you too." Sunshine holds back her tears.

"How are you guys?" I wipe my tears. "You lost her- You guys never said anything... I get it, she was my girlfriend, but she was your best friend too, your sister, all of you. If it's this hard for me, I can't even imagine how hard it is for you guys."

They all bow their heads. Antonia and Sunshine are the first to weep; Chanse tries to be strong, but his eyes are overflowing with tears. *Let it out, brother.* Aura and Celeste hold each other's hands and grieve. I feel the weight of their loss, our loss because I didn't even realize that I prepared an extra plate for Kelsey. All of them stayed strong, hiding their grievances to protect me, but that only kept the pain in. But today, we mourn for our best friend.

I bow my head, the tears slowly coming back. I feel a hand on my shoulder, and it's Celeste's; I hug her, letting out all the pain. Antonia and Aura get up and hug me as well. Chanse follows and embraces us. I glance at Sunshine, and she's still weeping with her head down. This is especially hard for Sunshine; Kelsey was her best friend in our group of best friends. They were the ones who knew each other in elementary.

I grab her shirt and pull her towards us, and we all cry together. *Let it all out, guys.*

∞

I step into the shower, and the water pours all over me as I stand still. Kelsey's dead; she's dead. This is true; this is my reality. I always wondered why everyone gave me that look when I attended work the next day. In my head, their condolences were sorry for the breakup. I wish that was it, but the fact that, for six months, I lived in that twisted reality makes everything so much shittier. I'm so empty, but after the whole breakfast fiasco, I feel my best friends filling up my cup.

I have to be strong and keep fighting, for Kelsey's memory. She'd hate seeing me the way I am now. I get out of the shower and borrow Celeste's oversized white T-shirt.

"Are you sure you're ready for this?" Chanse asks again.

"Yeah, it's time." I stare at all of them. They all look back at me, and I crack a smile. "Thanks again, bro, for driving last night."

"Bitch, thank you. You saved us money from getting an Uber." He tosses me the keys.

Appa was Kelsey's first baby. She gave me Appa when she bought her new car. Appa got me and Kelsey through many tough times. All the fights, all the sorrows, and all the love. Appa took us to all the places we couldn't go. I'm driving; it only makes sense I get everyone there. I connect my phone to the radio via Bluetooth and play our group song.

Everyone jolts up as they hear the first second of the music, and I smile, waiting for the lyrics to come.

Run fast from my day job, runnin' fast from the way it was.

We all sing along. *Slowly, they fill up my cup.* We stop by my house, and I quickly grab some things. I mean, I should have changed as well, but I don't care about that right now. After my house, we stop by a store on the way to where we were going.

We get to our destination, and everyone leaves the car except for me. "I'm here, baby," I said softly. My heart starts to beat faster but I'm not alone in this. I look ahead and see my Originals all waiting for me. I turn off the car and head out to them. We're all here, Kels; sorry it took a while. For all of us, this is the first time we're visiting her grave.

It was hard for all of them, with me checking out, they couldn't see her without me. The girls bought flowers. Chanse bought candles. I got a picture of Kels and me from the trip we took in Oregon, the one where we asked a hobo to take a picture of us, and he charged me twenty bucks for it. I also brought the picture of the Originals back in middle school.

We clean her gravestone and place the flowers next to it. Aura lights up the candles, and I put the picture frames down. We all stare at her, slowly succumbing to our pain. We huddle up and start crying. Finally, we all can properly mourn. We end up having a picnic with Kels and reminisce on the times we had with her. Some expressed the more personal moments with Kelsey that they didn't have to say, but I appreciate them telling their stories.

As the day neared its end, we say our goodbyes to Kels, until we see her again. We too made a pact to never hide our feelings from each other because when Kelsey was around, she never did that with any of us. We head out, and I drop everyone home one by one. This day has been a marathon of emotions, too much for me to deal with. The drive back home was pleasant. The sunset shined a little differently today, the air blew its calm winds a little differently today, and I feel a little different today.

I don't have to bear all of this alone anymore; if I didn't have any of them, I think I would have followed Kels, and she would hate me for that. I park the car in front of my house. I open the door, and the stench of trash piling up and dishes that haven't been washed enters my nose. *Is this my house?* This is not the home Kelsey and I made. Kels and I bought this house with everything we had and I was working on buying a ring for her in the next few years. I'm sorry, Kels.

I push all the piled mail on the floor to the side for now. I take my Air Pods from my work desk and begin cleaning. I throw my clothes in the laundry and nakedly clean the house. I can hear Kelsey screaming at me for always being naked around the house.

Four hours later, I managed to clear the tornado that hit my room, washed all my clothes, and threw out all the trash, five bags of them. I take my freshly dried pajama bottoms and wear them. Clothes don't need to be worn inside the house. I head out to the trash bin and throw out all the remaining depression that I was stuck in.

My neighbors see me and smile big, waving at me. I haven't seen Kenny and Albert in months, so happy to see them together. They were the first to greet Kelsey and me when we moved in.

I wave in return. The door shuts behind me and I notice all the mail I pushed to the side. I pick them up and go through them. Phone bills, letters from her work, and all these things I will go through later. I throw them on the table, and an envelope drops on the floor. My head tilts as I pick it up, "From me?"

∞

THE LETTER

The chair screeches as I drag it out from under the dining table. I tear open the envelope, and inside is a single piece of paper. I glance at the back of it, recognizing my own handwriting. I don't recall ever writing a letter to myself; then again, this must be a part of the memory loss. I pull out the paper, and to my shock, it's a page from my journal. I rise from my seat and make my way to my room, searching through the closet for my journal that I haven't laid eyes on in years. The page number from the letter is ninety-three, and coincidentally, that's the page of the journal I'm holding right now.

I confirm this is mine because it was custom-made by Kelsey. She drew all the page numbers on it. I furrow my brows and start reading:

Dear Sky,

It's me—well, you. Before I delve into everything, I'm not entirely sure if this will work, but here I am, writing to you. A decade ago, the version of "me" from back then, also known as you. I suppose this could be my way of finally closing that chapter in my life. You see, Sky, the day I learned about Kelsey's passing, a part of me died within. She was my other half for the longest time, and she still is. Much has unfolded since then, but I won't spoil the entirety of your future for you.

You might be enduring that heart-wrenching moment at this very instant, but I want you to know, it does get better. I am living each day because you chose to live and strive for a better life. Our friends are thriving; just yesterday, we enjoyed brunch in Paris. You've transformed our lives in profound ways, and I want to express my gratitude for being resilient on behalf of both of us. You're living right here where I am now. We even find love again, a prospect you once thought unimaginable.

Now, how does all of this work? I'm here in New Orleans, Albatross. There's a renowned lady who specializes in helping people let go of things. She assured me that she can deliver any message I want to my past self, and I chose your current moment because I remember how challenging it was for me, and I can only imagine how much more difficult it is for you. I hope this letter reaches you and serves as a reminder that things truly do improve. I wish for you to live the best life possible because that's what Kelsey wanted for us. I understand you might be grappling with the concept of time intricacies, as I did.

It took me a while to muster the courage to give this a shot. The lady explained that whatever impact the note has on its destination won't affect the present here, as it's a different point in time. In simpler terms, it's like the multiverse. So, consider this a potential future, one you can choose to live out if you wish, and it will be.

You are more than you think you are. I know because I am you.

Make peace with what happened, take the time to process it all, and when you're ready, release it all and breathe again. You deserve that much. I love you, man.

Love,
Sky

Today has been a waterfall of tears, but now I'm just lost in these emotions. I've been reading that letter over and over, trying to wrap my head around it. What does it mean for my future and my past? I wander around the living room, going through the words I wrote to myself, contemplating what these letters could really do.

"They can't change anything in the present, but they can alter things in the past... like six months ago," I mutter to myself. Grabbing my journal, I start jotting down a message to myself from ten months before the accident. I'm trying to explain how this whole thing works and how we might be able to save Kelsey. Maybe she can live in some other universe, enjoying life with the Originals until they're old and grey. My face is stained with the remnants of my tears. I can make things right; I can save Kelsey. I sign my name and slip the note into a fresh envelope.

On the back, I scrawl:

FROM ME.

About the Author

Photo by Rhoana Lynn Hendrix

Step into the vibrant world crafted by Victor Cabinta, a Filipino-American wordsmith nestled in the heart of Guam. Since childhood, he wove tales, harboring an emotional dream of becoming an author. Now, with a Bachelor's in English Literature and soon be a Creative Writing Master's graduate, Victor aspires to transcend borders, sharing his narratives globally, a tapestry rich with Filipino heritage and Guam's cultural hues. Awaiting the journey towards a Ph.D. in Creative Writing, Victor's literary voice resonates with diverse hues. Beyond the written word, he has graced the dance floor since 2010, showcasing his art professionally during college. When not immersed in the dance of words or body, Victor finds solace in capturing life's moments with loved ones by the beach, all while harmonizing with the tunes of Taylor Swift. Embark on this literary odyssey, where Victor Cabinta invites you to explore the intersections of culture, dance, and the timeless melodies of storytelling.

Printed in the USA
CPSIA information can be obtained
at www.ICGtesting.com
LVHW020834300124
770120LV00053B/1267